The
Tale
of
Benjamin
Bunny

FREDERICK WARNE

Published by the Penguin Group
Penguin Books Ltd, 27 Wrights Lane, London W8 5TZ, England
Penguin Putnam Inc., 375 Hudson Street, New York, N.Y. 10014, USA
Penguin Books Canada Ltd, 10 Alcorn Avenue, Toronto, Ontario, Canada M4V 3B2
Penguin Books (NZ) Ltd, Private Bag 102902, NSMC, Auckland, New Zealand
Penguin Books India (P) Ltd, 11 Community Centre, Panchsheel Park, New Delhi 110 017, India
Penguin Books (South Africa) (Pty) Ltd, 5 Watkins Street, Denver Ext 4, 2094, South Africa

Penguin Books Ltd, Registered Offices: Harmondsworth, Middlesex, England

Visit our web site at: www.peterrabbit.com

This edition first published by Frederick Warne 2001

1 3 5 7 9 10 8 6 4 2

Additional illustrations by Colin Twinn and Alex Vining

Colour reproduction by Saxon Photolitho
Printed and bound in Singapore by Tien Wah Press

The
Tale
of
Benjamin
Bunny

Based on the original tale
BY BEATRIX POTTER

FREDERICK WARNE

This is the tale of
Benjamin Bunny.

One morning he sat on
a bank in the woods.

Benjamin Bunny saw a cart on the road. Mr and Mrs McGregor were in the cart. They were going out for the day.

Benjamin ran off to tell his cousin, Peter Rabbit.

As he peered behind a tree, Benjamin saw two little ears sticking out.

It was his cousin, Peter
Rabbit, wrapped in a red
handkerchief.

Benjamin sat beside
Peter. "Peter, who has got
your clothes?"

Peter told him that
he had been chased
round the garden by
Mr McGregor and had
dropped his coat and
shoes.

Mr McGregor was using
them for a scarecrow!

"Come along, Peter," said Benjamin. "Mr and Mrs McGregor have gone out in their cart. Let us go and find your clothes."

Benjamin and Peter stood on the garden wall.

They could see Peter's shoes and coat on the scarecrow. There was a big green hat on the scarecrow too.

Benjamin and Peter
climbed down a pear
tree into the garden.
Peter fell down ... but
he was not hurt.

Peter put on his blue
coat and Benjamin put
on the green hat. It was
much too big for him!

Then Benjamin and
Peter collected onions
for Peter's mother.
They put them in the
red handkerchief.

As they walked through
the garden, Benjamin
munched on a lettuce
leaf.

But Peter Rabbit felt
very scared in
Mr McGregor's garden.
He was so scared that he
dropped the onions.

As Benjamin and Peter tried to find their way out of the garden, they were watched by some brown mice.

Suddenly, the little
rabbits stopped ...

This is what they saw—
a cat!

They hid underneath a basket. The cat walked over to the basket and …

She sat down on top
of it!

The cat sat there for
a very long time.
Benjamin and Peter were
very scared.

On the wall above the cat, Benjamin's father, old Mr Bunny, was smoking a pipe. He was looking for his son.

Old Mr Bunny jumped
down from the wall
and pushed the cat off
the basket.

Then he took the red
handkerchief of onions
and marched those
naughty rabbits home.

That night, the onions
were hung in the kitchen,
and Peter and his sister,
Cotton-tail, folded up the
red handkerchief.